The Sleeping Beauty

A Journey to the Ballet of the Mariinsky Theatre

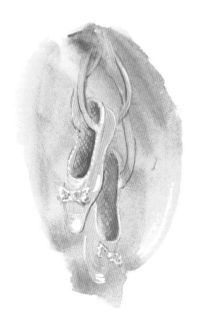

ACKNOWLEDGMENTS

Many people had a hand in ensuring the successful outcome of this project. We would like to thank the following people and institutions for their generous assistance and unfailing support at each and every sage: Jaqui Lividini, Ken Smart, The Mariinsky Foundation of America, Rita Z. Mehos, Stephen R. de Angelis, Costa Pilavachi, Mary Dinaburg, Ekaterina Sirakanian, Svetlana Shabanova, Natalia Metelitsa, Sarah DeKay, Ima Ebong, Tanya Ross-Hughes, David Hughes, and Thomas Hau.

— The Editors

The Houghton Library of Harvard College has generously given permission for the adaptation of the following work: "The Sleeping Beauty in the Wood," in *Histories, or tales of past times* by Charles Perrault. Translated from the French text by Robert Samber. London: J. Pote and R. Montagu, 1729. The volume is the first edition of Perrault's fairytales in English and the sole recorded copy of the work in existence.

First published in 2002 by

Glitterati Incorporated
New York | London

New York Office:
322 West 57 Street #19T
New York, New York 10019
Telephone 212 362 9119

London Office:
1 Rona Road
London NW3 2HY
Tel/Fax +44 (0) 207 267 9479

www.GlitteratiIncorporated.com
media@glitteratiincorporated.com for inquiries

First edition, 2002
Second printing, 2013

Library of Congress Cataloging-in-Publication data is available from the publisher.

Hardcover edition ISBN 13: 978-0-9721152-0-9

Design by Hotfoot Studio

Printed and bound in China
10 9 8 7 6 5 4 3 2

The Sleeping Beauty

A Journey to the Ballet of the Mariinsky Theatre

illustrated by Nikita Polyansky

A Journey to the Ballet of the Mariinsky Theatre
by Ima Ebong

The Sleeping Beauty adapted by Ima Ebong from the Mariinksy Theatre libretto
by Ivan Alexandrovich Vsevolozhsky and Marius Petipa, and from
Robert Samber's 1729 translation of *The Sleeping Beauty in the Wood* by Charles Perrault

Glitterati
INCORPORATED

New York | London

Lena-Gabrielle could not have been happier. It was Christmas Eve and she had just finished opening all of her presents. She lined them up against the window so that she could take everything in. Her favorite was a beautiful doll dressed in a pink ballet costume wearing shiny satin slippers. Lena-Gabrielle loved ballet and wanted to become a ballet dancer more than anything else in the world. She especially loved to practice twirling in front of the mirror. While playing, Lena-Gabrielle was all ears as she overheard the grown-ups talk excitedly about a new ballet called *The Sleeping Beauty*, which was to be performed at the famous Mariinsky Theatre on Christmas day. Lena-Gabrielle heard them say it was magical. 'Can we go?' asked Lena-Gabrielle, who loved ballet. 'Hrrumph' said her father, 'there's not a ticket to be had in all of Petersburg. I'll bet not even the stage mice could squeeze their way in.' Later that evening with her new doll

propped up at the end of her bed Lena-Gabrielle thought about the magical *Sleeping Beauty* ballet. She made up her mind to go. The next afternoon dressed in her best winter coat, and wearing her best hat and gloves she set out with her favorite new doll to see *The Sleeping Beauty*.

Lena-Gabrielle looked down at her little footsteps in the snow as she walked through St. Petersburg. Although she had gone shopping with her mother many times, and had driven through the city with her father, everything suddenly looked larger than she had ever seen. Lena-Gabrielle walked through a giant archway and saw the amazing Winter Palace. She had never seen it this close before. It looked like a green and white cake with gold icing decorations, the palace seemed to stretch out for miles, there must have been a thousand windows. Lena-Gabrielle crossed the courtyard and came to a giant statue of a man, who seemed to concentrate very hard while holding up part of a building on his shoulders. He was one of the ten Atlas brothers, famous in all of St. Petersburg for their strength. Her father had pointed them out to her many times before. 'Hello little girl' the statue said. Lena-Gabrielle looked startled and threw her head all the way back, so she could see his face. 'I'm going to the Mariinksy Theatre to see the ballet perform *The Sleeping Beauty*,' Lena-Gabrielle said, hoping that he might show her the way. 'I can see it all the way from here; you'll have to turn around and keep walking until you come to the bridge.' Lena-Gabrielle said thank you to Mr. Atlas, although she was not too sure which bridge he meant. There seemed to be so many bridges in St. Petersburg.

She walked towards the first bridge she saw. It had a pair of lions with golden wings guarding the entrance. 'Do you know the way to the Mariinsky Theatre?' Lena-Gabrielle asked, 'I'm going to see the ballet perform *The Sleeping Beauty*.' 'Oh dear' said one of the lions, 'I do not have a clue, I don't get around much, but you might try to ask that man over there in the fancy top hat and cape; he's clearly dressed for something, and besides I heard him whistle a pretty tune.' Lena-Gabrielle thanked the lion and went over to the man. She tugged on his cape and he turned around. He looked a bit like Father Christmas because he had a beard and a moustache that curled up on either side and had big round eyes. 'Hello little girl' he said. Lena-Gabrielle asked him 'Do you know the way to the Mariinsky Theatre?' 'As a matter of fact I do. I'm on my way there to see what they've made of my music. I wrote every single note for *The Sleeping Beauty* ballet, you know.' Together they walked across the bridge while Lena-Gabrielle told Mr. Tchaikovsky all about her plans to become a famous ballerina. He was so impressed that he offered not only to introduce her to Mr. Petipa, the famous ballet master, but also to take her on a tour of the theater before the performance.

Lena-Gabrielle could feel the excitement in the air as she walked. She had never seen so many ballet dancers in her life. In the middle of them all was a tall thin man. Everyone stopped and listened whenever he spoke. He must be very important, Lena-Gabrielle thought to herself. 'This,' Mr. Tchaikovsky said, pointing at the man with his cane, 'this is Mr. Petipa.' 'He is the magician responsible for making my notes leap off the page and dance.' Mr. Petipa swooped down and gently shook Lena-Gabrielle's hand. 'Mr. Tchaikovsky tells me you are going to be a famous ballerina when you grow up.' Before Lena-Gabrielle could say a word, Mr. Petipa snapped his fingers and a man appeared carrying the most beautiful pair of ballet shoes she had ever seen. 'These, young lady, once belonged to my daughter Maria, who is dancing tonight. I give them to you.' Lena-Gabrielle was thrilled. She could hardly wait to tell her parents. Lena-Gabrielle parted the beautiful velvet curtains and walked out on to the stage. She could hardly believe the sight. It was the biggest space Lena-Gabrielle had ever seen. She stared out at all the blue velvet seats and looked up at the balconies rising up and up and up, nearly all the way to the ceiling. She felt very tiny indeed. As Lena-Gabrielle turned back around to see the stage, the huge blue and gold curtains parted. It was so quiet, you could hear a pin drop. She clutched her favorite doll tightly. The magic was about to begin . . .

"There was once upon a time,

a king and a queen who were so sorry that they had no children, so sorry that it was beyond expression. They went to all the waters in the world, vows, pilgrimages, everything was tried and nothing came of it. At last however the queen had a beautiful baby daughter and the good King Florestan and his queen named her Aurora. To celebrate this happy occasion there was a very fine christening and the king instructed Lord Catalabutte, his Master of Ceremonies, to invite all the fairies they could find in the kingdom that they might become Aurora's fairy godmothers. Lord Catalabutte found seven fairies in all the kingdom; There was Lilac Fairy, who became Aurora's leading godmother; also invited was Fairy Canary, Fairy Violente, Breadcrumb Fairy, Fairy Candide, the fragrant Wheat flower Fairy, and the strange Fairy Carabosse.

Carabosse

14

Candide

Breadcrumb

Wheat-flower

Lilac

Canary

Violente

After the christening ceremony, all the guests entered the king's palace, where a great feast was prepared in honor of the fairies. There was placed before every one of them a magnificent golden dome cover. Placed underneath was a spoon, knife and fork, all of pure gold set with diamonds and rubies. As everyone was seated for dinner, they saw the old Fairy Carabosse angrily striding down the grand hall. Lord Catalabutte, the king's Master of Ceremonies, had forgotten to invite her to the dinner.

The king realized that she did not have a seat, and quickly ordered her a place setting but could not give her a magnificent gold dome cover as the other fairies had received. No matter how hard the king tried to apologize, no matter what he said to placate Carabosse, the damage had been done. The old fairy felt slighted and muttered some threats between her teeth. The king and queen were very concerned that this mistake would cost them dearly, and bring much unhappiness to their little princess. The kind and wise Lilac Fairy, who sat next to old Carabosse, heard her angry curses, and suspected that she might seek revenge by giving the baby princess some unhappy gift. As soon as the guests rose from table the Lilac Fairy hid herself behind the hangings, so that she might speak last, to repair as much as she possibly could the evil that the old fairy might do to Princess Aurora.

In the meantime all the fairies lined up and began to give their gifts to the princess. The youngest gave Aurora the gift of beauty, that she should be the most beautiful person in the world; the next, that she should have the wit of an angel; the third, that she should have an admirable grace in everything she did; the fourth, that she should dance perfectly; the fifth, that she should sing like a nightingale; and the sixth, that she should play all kinds of music to the utmost perfection. The old Fairy Carabosse's turn came next, and with great spite she waved her magic wand over Princess Aurora's cradle and declared that the princess would have her hand pierced with a spindle and die of the wound. At this very instant the Lilac Fairy came out from behind the hangings and assured the king and queen, that Aurora would not die but would instead fall into a deep sleep for one hundred years. The king, wishing to avoid the misfortune foretold by the old Fairy Carabosse, issued a decree banning everyone in the kingdom, on pain of death from using a spindle, or having any spindles in their houses.

The years passed by, Princess Aurora had a happy childhood. She grew up to be a beautiful young lady with many suitors—among them four handsome princes who each carried a medallion portrait of the lovely princess wherever they went, in the hope that one of them might one day marry the princess.

On Aurora's twentieth birthday, the king decided to give his daughter a grand birthday celebration in the hope that she might meet and fall in love with the prince of her choice. On the day of the ball Princess Aurora made a great entrance, accompanied by her maids of honor carrying bouquets and wreaths.

The four princes, struck by her beauty, rivaled each other for her attention. They all clustered around Aurora and urged her to dance, for it was rumored that she was the most graceful and entrancing dancer in the world. Wishing to please them, Aurora danced to the accompaniment of violins. The four princes were delighted, and wishing to please them even more, Aurora's steps became lighter and more graceful with each turn. She not only captivated the princes, but also the whole court as well as the assembled villagers who followed her ethereal steps as she spun around the ballroom.

Out of the corner of her eye Aurora
glimpsed an old woman marking time
with a spindle; carried away by the music,
she snatched the spindle from the old
woman and continued to dance with it
playfully, at one moment pretending it was a
scepter, and at another turn imitating the work
of a spinner. Suddenly she stopped dancing,
and in horror lurched forward and back-
ward in great pain as realized that she
had pierced her hand with the spindle.

The old woman from whom Aurora had taken the spindle threw off her cloak. It was the evil Fairy Carabosse. Immediately the four princes drew their swords and rushed towards the evil Fairy, but Carabosse—with a diabolical laugh—simply vanished into thin air, leaving a huge puff of smoke behind her.

Aurora was gently placed on a bed all embroidered with gold and silver; one would have taken her for a little angel, she was so very beautiful. Her fall had not diminished her complexion one bit; her cheeks were carnation, and her lips like coral; her eyes were shut, but they heard her breathe softly, which satisfied them that she was not dead. The king commanded that no one was to disturb her, but let her sleep quietly till she woke up. The good fairy approved every thing the good king had done; but as she had very great foresight, she thought the princess would awake and not know what to do with herself, being all alone in the old palace. To help her, she touched everything with her wand that was in the palace except the king and the queen. Immediately upon her touching them they all fell asleep, that they might be ready once again to be with the princess when she awoke. Even the very spits at the fire, full as they were of partridges and pheasants, also slept. All this was done in a moment; the good Fairy Lilac was very thorough and wasted no time

And now the king and the queen having kissed their child without waking her, left the palace, and put forth a proclamation that nobody should dare to come near it. This however was not necessary; for in a quarter of an hour's time there grew up all round about the park a vast number of trees, great and small, bushes and brambles intertwined with one another, so that no one could pass through: nothing could be seen, but the very top of the palace, and even that too, only from a long distance. The princess would have nothing to fear from the curious while she slept.

One hundred years later,

Prince Désiré, the son of the king then reigning, decided to go hunting near the forest covered castle. He soon grew tired and decided to stop by a riverbank to rest while he urged the rest of his hunting party to continue the hunt without him.

No sooner had they left, the prince saw a strangely beautiful sight; a luminous boat made of mother-of-pearl and precious stones, suddenly appeared on the river.

The Lilac Fairy, who also happened to be Prince Désiré's godmother, emerged from the boat and stepped ashore. All alone, the prince, who was forlorn at not yet finding a suitable bride, confessed to his godmother. None of the women in the kingdom had captured his heart, nor did he want to marry for duty instead of love. Touched by what she had heard, the Lilac Fairy waved her wand toward some cliffs in the distance to reveal an image of Aurora asleep in her bedchamber. The prince was immediately captivated and pleaded with the good fairy to take him to meet her.

Together they set off toward the castle where the princess lay sleeping. The journey took a night and a day. With each bend in the river they passed a forest of entangled trees on either side of the riverbank. Finally they reached the palace gates, which were so tall they appeared to touch the sky. At last, Prince Désiré came into a beautiful gold room, where before his eyes was the most beautiful sight he had ever seen. The Princess Aurora appeared a bright resplendent beauty who, although she had been asleep for a hundred years, had a luminous quality about her.

The prince approached, knelt down before her and gave her a kiss. And now the spell was broken. The princess awoke and looked at the prince tenderly.

The prince helped the princess to rise, and together they went into the great hall of mirrors, where they met the king and queen. The prince bowed to the king and queen, and asked permission to marry their daughter. The king gave his consent saying the words 'it is her destiny.' He joined the couple's hands and asked the royal chaplain to marry them in the palace chapel.

There was a fine procession from the magnificent esplanade to the great dining hall. The wedding party was led by the king and queen, who in turn were followed by the newly-weds and their retinue; including the Fairies of Diamonds, Gold, Silver and Sapphire. Behind the royal procession were hundreds of invited guests among them many famous names from the land of fairy tales. There was Bluebeard and his wife, Puss in boots, Goldilocks, Cinderella and Prince Charming, Beauty and the Beast, Tom Thumb and his brothers, and even Little Red Riding Hood who wore a beautiful red velvet cape. Everyone was there.

After the great feast, there was much dancing and merriment. The King's band played excellent music, even though they had not practiced for a hundred years. **"**

It was the day after Christmas. Lena-Gabrielle, still sleepy, opened her eyes slowly and looked around her bedroom. She tried very hard to remember everything from the night before; meeting Mr. Atlas, then Mr. Tchaikovsky, and the magnificent stage at the Mariinsky Theatre. 'Did it all really happen to me?' She thought to herself. She looked for her favorite doll, which rested by her pillow. In her hand she held ballet shoes. 'Where did they come from?' Lena-Gabrielle wondered, 'Was it all just a beautiful dream?'